Bernie and the Smelly Cheese Balls

Stay true!
-Jules

This is a book published by Steel Pen Publishing

Send inquiries to:

Steel Pen Publishing
PO Box 3118
Easton, PA 18043

Please visit our website at:
Steelpenpublishing.com

ISBN 978-0-9906639-0-4

Printed in the United States of America
By
United Book Press, INC
1807 Whitehead Road
Baltimore, MD 21207

December 2014

This book is dedicated to my family, as well as the students and teachers who have inspired my work in the Allentown School District.

Chapter 1

It was the first day of school for eight year-old Bernie. As she stepped out of her yellow row home she could hear the honks of trucks and music coming from the cars. The busy street sounded different now that school started, especially during the morning rush hour. It was louder and busier now.

Bernie could also feel the nervousness in her stomach. This year, Bernie hoped to make new friends. In her hand was her favorite blue lunch box. Her mother waited at the door as Bernie stepped off the porch.

She turned to her mom and told her, "*Eb shoofeek bayed el madrase.*" (I will see you after school).

Her mother said, "*Koonay shotra.*" (Do a good job).

Bernie blew her mother a *bous* (kiss) and waved good-bye. Her mother stood behind the glass of the door, watching Bernie step down the porch. Bernie's mother was just as nervous as Bernie on the first day of school. She worried a lot about Bernie because Bernie was very shy at school and often had difficulty making new friends.

As she walked down the street of her friendly neighborhood, she wondered if she would make new friends this year. Bernie was born shortly after her parents moved to the United States. Her father called her his American surprise, his "gift" for coming to America.

Bernie grew up speaking Arabic at home, but spoke English at school. The only student that was at her school who was from the same country as her was in kindergarten, so Bernie didn't have any close friends who were like her.

Even though Bernie spoke a second language, she often thought she was the same as the other kids. She liked to play the same games, she watched the same TV shows, and she dressed in the same clothes.

Bernie felt different sometimes because her family didn't speak English very well, and sometimes ate different foods. She also felt awkward at school because of what her mother packed for her in her favorite blue lunch box. Most days her mother sent her to school with traditional Arabic foods, like a *labne* sandwich (creamy cheese spread on pita bread) or a *smaboousk* (bread pocket filled with meat).

As she thought about what made her so different at school she noticed that her favorite blue lunch box was a little heavier than usual. Bernie hoped her mother surprised her with a special treat, like a peanut butter and jelly sandwich or perhaps a chocolate chip cookie.

As she walked along the street, she waved to old Mr. Azar who was reading his newspaper.

"*Marhaba*" (hello), she cheerfully shouted.

"*Sabaah al-khayr*" (good morning), he replied.

Mrs. Ammary, who was one of the oldest women in the neighborhood, was sweeping her porch like she normally did every day. She asked Bernie, "*Wayn erneek*?" (Where is your mother).

Bernie replied, "*Bil bayl*." (At home).

Mrs. Ammary was known to be a great baker. She would often bake her own *khubz* (bread). That morning Bernie could smell the freshly baked bread coming from Mrs. Ammary's house.

As Bernie walked to school, she realized that she loved the

smells that floated throughout her neighborhood. The aromas of *toom* (garlic) from 2nd Street Pizza Shop or *the gahwa* (coffee) from the Grant Café. All of these smells reminded her of the yummy smells that came from own mother's kitchen.

There was just one smell that she couldn't stand; a smell that would forever change her life.

Chapter 2

As Bernie disappeared from her mother's view, on her way to school, she imagined her mother was probably headed back into the kitchen to check on a fresh pot of milk boiling on the stove.

Bernie's mother loved to be in the kitchen. She enjoyed cooking meals for her family. Often the smell of garlic or different spices floated throughout the house. Bernie's mother made many different recipes including chicken and rice, spinach pies, and her favorite recipe to make, *shankeleesh* (cheese balls with spice).

The one scent that Bernie could not stand at all was the stink of the *shankeleesh*. She was disgusted by the stench of those smelly cheese balls. Everyone in her family ate the cheese balls. Everyone except Bernie! She absolutely hated the stench of those smelly cheese balls even though she knew her mother spent a lot of time preparing them.

Her mother would buy *haleeb* (milk), lots of milk, to prepare the smelly cheese balls. Sometimes Bernie would visit a local farmer with her mom to get milk to make the smelly cheese balls. Many times she wondered how she could rid her house of them.

Bernie would imagine hiding them around the house. She also thought she could knock them out of her house with a baseball bat. Or maybe she could drop them from the top window of her house to go SPLAT! Bernie even wrote a letter to her local dairy farmer begging him for help.

Dear Milk Farmer,

Please stop milking the cows. My mother uses your milk to make the smelly cheese balls. I do not like their smell. Please help me.

Sincerely Annoyed,

Bernie

One time, Bernie tried to hide the big silver pot her mother used to boil milk. Her plan didn't work. Even after hiding the big silver pot in the basement, Bernie's mother went out and bought a new one. Her mother ended up finding the old silver pot and now doubled the amount of *shankeleesh* she made, doubling the smell of cheese balls in the house!

Her mother was very proud of her cheese balls. All the neighbors loved the way she made them. She would even box them and give them as gifts to her family and friends. Her mother would try to feed everyone the smelly cheese balls.

Bernie could remember a time when her mother took Bernie to the doctor's office. Her mother even offered them to the doctor to thank him for helping Bernie get better after being sick.

"*Min fadlak ahkahl el shankleesh,*" (Please eat the smelly cheese balls), she told the doctor after shoving a ball and a piece of pita bread in front of him.

"Huh, okay, thanks, I guess," he replied awkwardly. How embarrassing that moment was for Bernie!

Chapter 3

When Bernie arrived at school, a new smell interrupted her thoughts of smelly cheese. The sweet smell of pizza being prepared in her school's cafeteria made her forget about the smelly cheese balls. She wished all cheese could smell as delicious as the mozzarella baking in the school's ovens.

"Good morning," she said to the 5th grade safety monitor who was watching the students enter the school.

"Third graders this way," the safety monitor replied pointing down the long hallway.

Bernie walked nervously to her classroom. Waiting outside was her new teacher.

"Hi, I'm Mr. Leonard, welcome to Room 112," her new 3rd grade teacher said.

Bernie was excited for the start of the school year, but she was also anxious, wondering if she would make new friends. Bernie wondered about her new teacher. She wondered if he was nice and if he was going to hand out stickers. Bernie also thought about her mother and how if she was here she would probably be pushing smelly cheese balls in front of Mr. Leonard.

Her teacher interrupted her thoughts, "Excuse me, do you speak English?" Bernie realized that she never responded to Mr. Leonard.

Bernie realized she was caught up in her thoughts of the smelly cheese balls. She quickly replied, "Yes, sorry, yes, good morning, my name is Bernie!"

Mr. Leonard pointed her to the inside of classroom, and instructed Bernie to find her name tag and seat. To Bernie's relief, there was no sign that her mother sent smelly cheese balls to her teacher. She didn't see them, nor did she smell them. What a relief!

As Bernie sat at her new desk,

a girl sat down next to her. Her nametag said Jenny.

Jenny had a new bookbag and a new lunch box too. Bernie imagined what Jenny's mother probably put in her lunch box- a ham and cheese sandwich, cream filled cookies, maybe even a juice box. Jenny's mom didn't make smelly cheese balls, Bernie thought.

As Bernie sat at her desk, flipping through her notebook, Jenny asked, "Hey, do you know what time lunch is?"

Bernie replied excitedly, "No, but I heard we might have art class today. I love art!"

Jenny agreed, "Me too, I love to do art projects. My name is Jenny, what's your name?"

"Bernie."

Both Bernie and Jenny smiled at each other and began to setup their desks. Mr. Leonard walked in and said, "okay boys and girls, we are ready to start. Please get out your pencils and crayons."

As Mr. Leonard was getting the front table organized, Bernie whispered to Jenny, "Hey, maybe we can sit together at lunch." Jenny nodded in agreement.

Bernie was excited. She was excited to start to a new school year. She was excited to have Mr. Leonard as her teacher. But most of all, she was excited to have made a friend.

Chapter 4

As Bernie sat in class, her mind wandered to her favorite blue lunch box sitting in the classroom closet. She was so eager to see what special snack her mom packed in her favorite blue lunch box and she couldn't stop thinking about what delicious food made her lunch box so heavy this morning.

She wondered if it was cookies or maybe those peanut butter crackers she loved so much. Perhaps her mother packed her a chocolate pudding cup. The clock hit 11:45 and Bernie knew it was time to head to the cafeteria.

"Okay boys and girls, grab your lunch boxes from the closet and line up quietly at the door," Mr. Leonard told the class.

Bernie quickly grabbed her favorite blue lunch box and headed to the line. Jenny stood in front of her. As the kids from her class walked into the loud cafeteria, with their lunch boxes, Bernie was wondering if she and Jenny would share their snacks and talk as friends.

Finally, Bernie sat down at her

classroom's lunch table. She looked around to see her classmates open their lunch boxes. Some children opened to find turkey sandwiches, some children took out vanilla pudding, and some children were even happy to discover fruit snacks in their lunch boxes.

The time finally came when Bernie could open her favorite blue lunch box to reveal what was weighing it down. When Bernie finally opened her lunch box, she didn't see fruit snacks, vanilla pudding, or even a turkey sandwich. To Bernie's horror, she found her worst nightmare!

Two big, gross, green, SMELLY CHEESE BALLS!

How could her mother do this to her? How could she put those smelly cheese balls in her favorite blue lunch box?!

Almost immediately, the horrid, reeking smell hit the air in the cafeteria. All the children sitting around her stopped eating their lunches and looked around to see what could possibly smell soooooo bad.

Bernie heard all the chatter of the cafeteria come to a screeching halt as her cheeks began to burn with shame.

All of the kids at her table suddenly looked disgusted, their faces scrunched up, some of them holding their noses as they stared at her and the awful, horrible surprise in her favorite blue lunch box.

Bernie didn't know what to do. If she cried, all the kids would laugh at her. If she ran away she wouldn't get to eat any lunch. Bernie knew what she had to do. She had to muster the courage to eat a piece of the smelly cheese balls.

Bernie swallowed the lump that was in her throat, picked up a smelly cheese ball, and took a bite, hoping not to get sick from the putrid aroma as she chewed the stinky cheese.

Having a smelly lunch was one thing, but getting sick all over the lunch table was a disaster she couldn't bear to imagine.

Chapter 5

Jimmy was a boy Bernie knew since 1st grade. He had been in her class every year, but he never spoke to her. Today, Jimmy was sitting next to her in the cafeteria. After Bernie took a bite of the smelly cheese he spoke his first words to Bernie with his nose crumpled, "Are you really going to eat that?"

Bernie didn't know how to reply. She had to think of something quickly. All the kids were staring at her. Bernie was the only Arabic kid in her class, the only one in her grade, and none of the other kids even knew what these cheese balls were. So she decided to lie.

"My mother makes these especially for me on important days at school, like test days, or like today, the first day of school. They help me to do well in school!" she shouted out.

"No way!" said Mary, one of the best students in class. She *never* spoke to Bernie. Bernie remembered that Mary always ate ham and cheese sandwiches on sliced, white bread every day in 2nd grade.

"Those smelly things are going to make you get good grades on tests?" asked John, a boy who was known for always getting into trouble for talking during tests.

Even Jenny, who Bernie thought was her new friend, was looking at her in confusion.

Jenny quietly asked her, "Did your mom really pack those for you so you could get good grades?"

Bernie knew she had told a lie, but it was too late to take it back now. So, against everything her parents had taught her about telling the truth, she continued.

Mary came and sat next to Bernie and asked her for a piece of the smelly cheese ball. She told Bernie that she had been reading a lot over the summer and she really wanted to score well on the upcoming reading tests.

Bernie reluctantly offered her

a bite, knowing that it wasn't the cheese. It was all of her hard work that made her a good student, but she didn't know how to get out of the lie.

Mary took a small bite, smiled weakly, and chewed a piece of the smelly cheese ball. Amazed, the other children started to talk and soon the entire cafeteria was buzzing about the smelly cheese balls. Kids started to crowd around her and Bernie began to divide up the cheese ball. The only thing left in her favorite blue lunch box was a few flakes of oregano and some crumbs of cheese.

Bernie thought that would be the end of it, and she could forget about the lie she told, but the kids in her class had other ideas.

<u>Chapter</u> <u>6</u>

A few days later Mary found out she almost had a perfect score on her reading test. Word began to spread about the amazing power of the smelly cheese balls. Every day at lunch, kids from all different classes were asking Bernie to bring the smelly cheese balls to school, in hopes that they would do well on their tests too.

"Hey, Bernie, do you have any

of the smelly cheese balls today?" asked Jimmy.

"No, I don't, why?" asked Bernie.

"I wanted to try them too. I want some for the spelling test tomorrow," said Jimmy.

"Well maybe I could bring some in tomorrow," said Bernie.

"If you bring me some, I promise to share my crayons with you tomorrow during art class," replied Jimmy.

As Bernie was sitting on a bench on the playground, another classmate asked for some smelly cheese balls and then invited her to a game of hopscotch.

As Bernie walked into the

cafeteria, another classmate asked her for some smelly cheese balls, then invited Bernie to sit with her group of friends during lunch.

Bernie was immediately excited. These girls never paid any attention to her before that day.

In the days that followed, Bernie was asked over and over again for the smelly cheese balls. She believed these kids really wanted to be her friends. Bernie's new popularity made her really happy.

Even Jenny the girl who liked to do art projects asked her one morning while walking into their classroom.

"Bernie, I was hoping that you could bring in some smelly cheese balls for my reading test on Friday. I really want to do well," Jenny said.

Before Bernie could even answer, Jenny added, "Hey, maybe then we can go skating on Saturday."

"Oh, okay, I will try," said Bernie.

Bernie really wanted to go skating, but she worried Jenny wouldn't want to go skating if she didn't help her with her test.

It seemed like everywhere Bernie went, whether it was in the cafeteria, al art class or on the playground, her classmates were asking her for smelly cheese balls.

Bernie never thought she would be friends with kids like Mary, Jimmy, and Jenny. She couldn't let them down. She had to get them the smelly cheese balls. Bernie kept thinking she would do anything to keep her new friends.

Now Bernie had a BIG problem. She wondered how she was going to sneak so many of the smelly cheese balls out of her house without her mom noticing their disappearance.

She needed a plan.

Chapter 7

The next morning and every morning for a week, Bernie would wake up early to pack a half dozen of the smelly cheese balls. She hid them in her bookbag.

One morning her mother opened the refrigerator and was puzzled as she looked through the plastic food storage container where she usually kept the smelly cheese balls.

"Bernie?" her mother said in questioning voice.

"*Naahm, emme,*" (Yes, mother), Bernie said nervously thinking her mother noticed the missing cheese balls.

"*Wayn el zaytoun?*" (Where are the olives), she asked.

"*Foh el berod,*" (Above the refrigerator), Bernie said feeling relieved.

"*Shukran,*" (Thank you), her mother replied.

Although Bernie felt guilty for taking them from her mom without asking, she believed she was doing a good thing. She felt all her classmates were accepting her for who she was, even though she had to give them something in return for their friendship. One day after Bernie filled her bookbag with the smelly cheese balls, she zipped it up and left it by the front door of her house. Her mother moved the bookbag to get started on cleaning the living room.

As her mother lifted the bookbag, she asked, "*Lay el baakeel laqeel?*" (why is your bookbag heavy)?

Bernie responded hesistantly, "*Kateer kutub, el mudarris eb tahtee kateer kutub,*" (lots of books, the teacher gives a lot of books).

"*Afhamet,*" (I understand), she said as she smiled and continued dusting.

Bernie tried to ignore the feelings she was having. She felt bad about not telling her mother the truth. However, Bernie was happy at school for the first time in her life.

Kids were picking her first for games in gym class and recess. The kids that always ignored her were now talking to her. She was also being asked to sit with the popular kids at lunch. She had more birthday party invitations than she could count.

Bernie's new friends were eating smelly cheese and taking their tests with false confidence. What they weren't doing was studying. In fact, it seemed like everyone was eating the smelly cheese.

Everyone except Paul.

Chapter 8

"Hey do those things really help?" Paul asked Bernie on the playground as they were collecting the sports equipment after recess.

Bernie had known Paul since Kindergarten, but they weren't really friends. Paul was one of the best kickball players in her grade. He was always captain and his team always won. Paul could kick the ball far enough to clear the fence of the school's playground. Paul never picked Bernie for his team and she knew why. Bernie often missed the ball when she tried to kick it. The two times she actually did kick it, the opposing team caught it.

Paul played basketball really well too. One time at recess he made ten foul shots in row. Even though he was good at sports, Paul didn't know his multiplication tables past the 6s, nor did he understand fractions very well.

"Well they seem to be working for everyone," replied Bernie. Bernie wondered if Paul was asking her about the smelly cheese balls because of the upcoming math test on fractions.

"Are you nervous about the fractions test?" asked Bernie.

"No," Paul started, "ok, yes, I am kinda nervous," he admitted. "Can you help me?".

Bernie responded, "Yes, when I come to school tomorrow, meet me by the third floor water fountain, and I will put one in your book bag."

Paul agreed and added, "Please, don't be late!"

Bernie thought that if she could help him score well on his test, maybe he would pick her for his kickball team.

The next morning Bernie had her usual collection of smelly cheese balls in her bookbag. The morning bell rang and Bernie raced up to the third floor water fountain to meet Paul. She found him pacing back and forth with his bookbag already opened.

"Where were you?" he growled. "I have been waiting for you and your stupid cheese balls!"

Bernie felt bad that Paul was so nervous, but he didn't understand that her mother was cleaning the refrigerator when she had to sneak the cheese balls into her bookbag.

"Here," she said, as she gave him the cheese ball.

"These better work!" he grumbled at her.

"They will," she said quietly. They both zipped up their bookbags and ran to their classroom.

As Bernie and her classmates were reviewing for the math test, Bernie had a strange feeling, especially when she looked at Paul. She felt anxious and she wasn't sure why she was feeling this way.

Finally, the time came for the fractions math test. Bernie thought that maybe she was just nervous. She decided to ignore that feeling and focus on the test. Bernie had studied her math notes, because she knew that the smelly cheese balls were no substitute for studying. Most of the kids in her class didn't realize that, and they had asked for smelly cheese balls this past week, hoping they would score well just by eating them.

Bernie found herself thinking about all of the invites she received to parties, how many times she was asked to sit next to everyone at lunch, and how many teams she was picked for at recess.

The students cleared their desks and got their pencils ready.

Mr. Leonard handed out the tests. At this point Bernie's heart was pounding. As she began to answer the questions, she noticed the other students in the class looking around the room at each other. Bernie thought they looked confused as they calculated their answers. As they finished their tests, they handed them to Mr. Leonard, smiling confidently at Bernie.

Bernie took a quick glance at Paul. As Paul was taking his test, she could see that he had hid the smelly cheese ball in his desk, nibbling at it after every few questions until he was finished.

Paul looked at her and smiled proudly thinking he probably got all the right answers. After he was done, he hid the smelly cheese ball back inside his desk and handed his test to Mr. Leonard. Paul thought he got a good grade, thanks to the smelly cheese ball. But Bernie had a feeling he probably didn't get a good grade.

Bernie had a feeling nobody got a good grade.

Chapter 9

The next day, Bernie's teacher, Mr. Leonard, handed back the fractions tests to the students, saying disappointedly, "Boys and girls, one student scored very well on the test, however, the rest of you did not and I am wondering why so many of you scored so low on the test. So we need to review strategies and you are going to take a retest on Friday."

All the students looked upset. They all expected to score well on the fractions test. They have been eating smelly cheese balls all week in hopes of getting good grades. They all thought that Bernie's method would help them.

Bernie froze in her seat. She wondered what happened on the tests. She couldn't help but wonder what would happen to all the invites, the lunch seats, and the recess games. She also wondered who the one person was who scored so high that he or she didn't have to retake the test.

Paul thought for sure it was him. So did Jimmy. So did Mary. So did Jenny.

"So boys and girls, I'm going to hand back the tests, so you can see which questions you got wrong and we can review those problems," Mr. Leonard told the class.

One by one, Mr. Leonard gave each student their test. As Bernie watched the look on her classmates' faces she knew they would be taking the test over. Bernie wanted to crawl under her desk and hide.

Mr. Leonard got to Bernie's desk and dropped off her test. An A! Bernie scored an A, but she was not excited because she realized she was the only one who didn't have to retake the test. Bernie was scared to look up at her classmates. Mr. Leonard's next announcement interrupted Bernie who was staring at her test.

"So Bernie, I'm happy to say that you will not have to retake the fractions test, good work! As for the rest of you, we will be reviewing fraction strategies, starting now. You will have extra homework this week and your re-test will be on Friday, so make sure you prepare for the it!" Mr. Leonard announced to the class.

All of Bernie's new friends shot her the angriest looks she had ever seen! The teacher patted Bernie on the back for her outstanding test score, making things worse.

Bernie realized that she never stopped studying, but it seemed that all the other students did.

"Liar!" shouted Jimmy.

"Fake!" screamed Mary.

"How could you do this Bernie?" questioned Jenny.

"Bernie and her smelly cheese balls didn't work!!" Paul yelled as he pulled out the smelly cheese ball, smashing it in his hand.

Chapter 10

Mr. Leonard looked shocked and confused. He wondered why all the students were shouting at Bernie after he announced the test scores. However, what was most puzzling to Mr. Leonard was why Paul had cheese in his hand.

"Paul, what is in your hand?" asked Mr. Leonard.

"She's a liar, a liar!" screamed Paul.

The rest of Bernie's classmates starting joining in with Paul's yells.

All Bernie could hear were the words, liar and fake. Bernie felt so bad about herself and what she did. She soon realized that everyone in the class was angry with her. Her plan for gaining friends is exactly what ended all her friendships.

"Paul, you need stop yelling and explain to me why you are calling Bernie a liar and why are you holding cheese in your hand?" Mr. Leonard asked a little louder.

"Mr. Leonard, Bernie gave out these cheese balls telling us that they would make us smart and help us score well on tests. She brought them from home and gave them out to the class. A lot of us ate them to get ready for the fractions test, so we didn't study. We all ended up with bad grades," explained Paul.

Mary agreed, "Bernie scored high on the fractions test because she studied. She knew that the smelly cheese balls wouldn't help her with the test!"

Mr. Leonard couldn't quite believe what he was hearing from his students. He turned to Bernie and asked, "Is this right, Bernie? Did you lie to all your classmates about the smelly cheese balls?"

Bernie didn't know how to answer her teacher. If she told him the truth her classmates would stop being friends with her. If she lied to him, she would have to prove to everyone that the smelly cheese balls work. She wished she could run away to another school and start all over.

"Hmmm…" Bernie replied while gulping a big lump in her throat, leaving her mouth dry. She looked around at everyone's faces. The whole class was staring at her. Bernie could feel her cheeks turning bright red. Her heart was pounding. Her hands were sweaty.

"Mr. Leonard, my mom packed two smelly cheese balls in my lunch box. I can't stand those cheese balls. Everyone wondered what they were, so instead of explaining what they really were, I ate them in front of everyone and told them the only reason my mom packed them in my lunch box was to make me smart at school," Bernie explained.

"Why did you lie about the cheese balls?" asked Mr. Leonard.

"I lied because I was too embarrassed. The cheese balls are a different kind of food. I didn't want the kids to think I was weird, so I told them my mom packed them in my lunch box so I would do well in school. I made it seem like it was a good thing," Bernie finally admitted to her teacher.

"Bernie, I still don't understand, how did you get all the cheese balls to the students at school?" asked Mr. Leonard.

Bernie didn't want to answer, but she knew she had to finally confess her plan.

She answered, "My mom makes them every other day. After she puts them in the refrigerator, I would steal a few at a time, by putting them into my bookbag. When I got to school, I would hand them out by the water fountain or at lunch time."

Mr. Leonard didn't know how to reply. He looked confused, and disappointed in Bernie.

Mr. Leonard wasn't the only one in the class who was upset. Bernie quickly scanned the classroom and could see the angry faces of her classmates.

Bernie put her head down in shame. She knew what she did was wrong.

Chapter II

Bernie soon found herself alone and sad waiting to see the principal.

Principal Peterson walked out of his office and invited Bernie to sit down. Bernie felt guilty as she walked into his office especially when she looked up to see her mother sitting in the other chair in front Principal Peterson's desk.

Bernie couldn't take her eyes off her mother. Her mother's eyes looked just like Mr. Leonard's did when she walked out of his classroom.

"Bernie, I have to admit, I am a little surprised to see you here in my office," Principal Peterson told her, making Bernie feel even more disappointed in herself. Bernie was usually a great student, who didn't get into trouble, especially with the principal.

Bernie was grateful that her mother couldn't understand what Principal Peterson was saying to her.

He continued, "Just so you know Bernie, when we called home, I had Mrs. Hanna translate everything to your mother."

Bernie now knew her mother

knew everything that she did.

"I know Principal Peterson. At first, I told the kids that my mom put the cheese balls in my lunch box on purpose because I was humiliated. I didn't want to be different from all the other kids. I lied to them and told them that the cheese balls would make me do well at school, but then-" she slowly stopped talking.

"But then, what, Bernie?" he asked.

"But then, the kids started to ask for the cheese balls so that they could do well on their tests. So I started to bring them in," she replied.

"Bernie, you stole the cheese balls from your mother," he said. Once Principal Peterson told her this, Bernie couldn't help but look at her mother.

"*Ana sratone, ya umma,*" (I stole them, mom), she told her mother.

Bernie's mother replied, "*Mnihnkay feeyah bahdan,*" (we will speak of it later). Bernie's mother gave a look that Bernie would never forget.

Bernie turned to Principal Peterson.

"Yes, I did. I stole them because I wanted to be popular. And I was popular! All the kids were inviting me to parties, and everyone was picking me first for games at recess. I wasn't sitting alone at lunch anymore," she continued.

"Bernie, you lied to your classmates, to your teacher, to your mother, and to yourself," he said to her.

"I know I lied, but it felt good to have friends, even if the friendships were fake," she admitted sadly.

"Bernie, if you were having trouble making friends, you could've talked to your teacher, me, our school counselor, or your parents. You didn't have to lie about who you were or what the cheese balls could do," he said softly.

He continued, "I think you need to go home and talk with your mother about all this and come back tomorrow, with a fresh perspective."

Bernie nodded, "Okay, Principal Peterson."

"You will have detention during recess for a week," he told her.

Bernie and her mother got up

from the chairs. Bernie's mother shook Principal Peterson's hand as he walked them out of his office.

Chapter 12

"*Ana arafet yhakday el shankeleesh* (I know you took the cheese balls)," her mother said as she and Bernie walked home.

Bernie didn't know what to say to her mother. She was embarrassed that she felt different from the other kids at school. She felt ashamed that she lied to be popular and tried to make friendships based on those lies.

Most of all she was worried about what her mother thought about her now after learning the truth.

Her mother said, "*halee binkour asloo, mahindoo asil* (he who denies who he is, comes from nothing)."

Bernie responded, "bes kan bedah yahon heboona (I just wanted them to like me)."

"*Mahb tareefah entay khassah?* (Don't you know how special you are?) Bernie's mom asked.

Bernie never felt special, until now. Her mother soon made her realize that the world is filled with people from all different cultures and backgrounds.

Bernie knew that her mother was always proud of her and she explained to Bernie that she should

be proud of who she was, even
if there are things that make her
different.

As Bernie walked home through
her neighborhood, she learned
a lesson about friendship. She
understood that if she wanted to
make real friends, who would always
be there for her, she shouldn't lie
to them, no matter how much she
wanted to be liked.

Real friends, thought Bernie, will
like you for who you are, not for what
you have packed in your favorite
blue lunch box.

Bernie looked at her mother
and knew she was right. Although
Bernie was grounded for two weeks
at home and had to serve detention
with Principal Peterson at recess
everyday for a week at school, she
didn't mind it. She knew that her

mother loved her and she would find true friends.

A few days later, Bernie was walking down the busy street, carrying her favorite blue lunch box. Jenny, the girl who loved to do art projects, came over to her when she reached the corner by their school. She forgave her for what happened and admitted she shouldn't have just relied on the smelly cheese balls for help, but she also should've studied. Jenny also reassured her that things would work out at school with the other kids.

"Hey, Jenny," said Mary, the smart girl in class, who ate ham and cheese sandwiches everyday.

Jenny replied pointing at Bernie, "Hey, Mary, this is Bernie, she is my friend and she loves to eat cheese!"

All the girls, including Bernie, smiled, and then burst out giggling!

The girls laughed a little more as they entered the playground. Then they started to talk about the upcoming social studies assignment at school. They planned to work together to complete the project.

As Bernie continued to walk into school with her new friends, she peeked into her favorite blue lunch box, smiled and knew it didn't matter what was inside.

Julie Saba

Author

Julie Saba is a first time author. She was born and raised in Allentown, Pennsylvania, where her parents settled after immigrating in 1977. One of seven children, Julie was the first child in her family to graduate from college. She graduated with a B.A. in Business Administration from Muhlenberg College. After becoming a mother, she returned to Muhlenberg to earn her Elementary Education Certification. After graduating she began to teach in the Allentown School District where she currently teaches 5th grade. Julie lives in the Lehigh Valley with her husband and two children.

Carla Rodrigues

Illustrator

Carla M. Rodrigues has been actively creating art
and designs for over 20 years while pursuing her
passion for elementary education. Originally from the
Azores, Portugal, Carla holds a B.A. in Graphic Design
from the University of Lisbon and both a B.A. and M.A
in Elementary and Special Education respectively
from East Stroudsburg University. She currently lives
in Eastern Pennsylvania with her husband and three
children where she works as a public school teacher.
This is Carla's second illustrated book. Please visit her
website www.carlasartstudio.com to learn more!